The Mystery of
the Pirate's Treasure

Earl Thomas

High Noon Books
Novato, California

Cover Design: Michael Cincotta
Interior Illustrations: Herb Heidinger

Special thanks to Bobby Stinnett and her reading classes at Christiansburg, VA, Middle School for much help with these books.

International Standard Book Number: 0-87879-534-0

9 8 7 6 5 4
4 3 2 1 0 9 8 7 6 5

You'll enjoy all the High Noon Books. Write for
a free full list of titles.

Contents

CHAPTER 1

Gold Fever

Carlos Mendez and P.J. Turner were riding home from work in Carlos's old car. They were talking about a library book.

"Did that book really say that a lot of gold is buried in the city park?" P.J. asked.

"No. It just tells some old stories about pirate treasure buried near here," Carlos said.

"Does it give any clues?" P.J. asked.

"Clues about what?" Carlos asked.

"About where the gold was buried," P.J. said.

"The best thing is for you to read the book. I'll bring it tomorrow," Carlos said.

Carlos parked his car in the lot in front of the old Westside Apartments.

1

They got out and walked in different directions to get to their family apartments.

The next day after work P.J. started to read the book. After a few minutes he forgot the other people and the noise from the TV set. He was very interested in Chapter 3, "Pirates Visit Major City."

That chapter told how pirates had come to the area long before Major City was even there.

Another paragraph read,

"An old story says that the treasure was buried just off the main trail through this area. It was buried in two places. Most of the treasure was buried halfway between a very large gray rock and a group of red oak trees. The pirate leader, Red Eye Perez, said he would come back and get the gold. Nobody knows if he ever did. People have looked but no one has ever found the treasure."

The next day Carlos and P.J. talked again at lunch.

"What do you think about the treasure, Carlos?" P.J. asked.

Carlos said, "I think it's still there."

"I'm not so sure," P.J. answered. "But if it is, do you think we can find it? That's a very big park. That gold was buried more than 200 years ago."

Carlos smiled. "Yes, I think the gold is still there. And I think we can find it."

P.J. did not reply right away. He started to tap his fingers. Then he said, "Carlos, that book about the treasure was printed 40 years ago. In 40 years how many people would have searched for the gold?"

Carlos replied, "Hundreds!"

P.J. smiled at him. "I don't believe any treasure is still there. In fact, we don't really know if there *ever* was any."

Carlos stood up. "Well, will you help me

look for it? That's the only way to be sure."

P.J. picked up his lunch pail. "O.K. I'll help. We'll talk about it later. Right now we've got to get back to work."

They picked up their lunch boxes and walked back inside the Watson Furniture Company where they both worked.

CHAPTER 2

Trouble!

On Saturday P.J. and Carlos went to the park. The day was sunny. The woods were green. A few wild flowers bloomed on the ground.

They rode the park bus as far as it went. Then they walked along the dim trails. The trails seemed to wind forever through the woods.

From time to time P.J. stopped walking. He stood and listened. Now and then he looked back along the trail.

He said softly, "I think someone is following us. Every time we stop, they stop. Every time we move forward, they move forward. I just looked over my shoulder. It looks like Bruno Jones and Mac Blum. Do you remember them from school?"

Carlos said, "I sure do. Why would they be following us?"

"I don't know," P.J. said.

"What shall we do?" Carlos asked.

P.J. looked down the trail. Then he said, "Let's hide behind those bushes. We can watch and see if they are really following us. Come on!"

They stayed on their knees behind the bushes for many minutes before they heard someone coming closer.

The first person they saw was Bruno Jones. He moved slowly along. He looked angry,

P.J. whispered, "Why should Bruno be angry? Do you think he is following us to learn what we know about the treasure?"

"Is Mac the only person with him?" Carlos asked.

"I don't see anybody else," P.J. whispered.

Mac walked up. He said to Bruno loudly,

"Where are they?"

"Don't talk so loud. They may be close by," Bruno said.

Bruno and Mac looked down the trail trying to see P.J. and Carlos. They looked to the sides of the trail. They looked right at the place where P.J. and Carlos were hiding in the bushes.

P.J. and Carlos did not move or speak.

Finally Bruno and Mac moved on along the trail. As soon as they were out of sight, P.J. and Carlos walked quickly back to the main part of the park.

When they got back to the bus stop, the little blue park bus came along and took them to the parking lot.

P.J. said as they walked toward Carlos's car, "We must be very careful with those two. They are real mean guys."

"I wonder if there is a back way to get into the park. Is there a gate back there?" Carlos wondered.

P.J. said, "I don't know but I think we had better find out!"

Carlos started his car. They both had a lot to think about as they drove home.

CHAPTER 3

One Hundred Dollars!

The next Saturday P.J. and Carlos went to see Mr. Bent, the park manager.

Mr. Bent told them that the back of the park had a heavy fence around it. The large gate was always locked.

"Nobody can get in back there unless they have a key or climb that high fence," Mr. Bent said.

"Will you give us an O.K. to come through that back gate?" P.J. asked.

Mr. Bent smiled. "You boys want to look for gold?"

"Yes, but how did you know?" P.J. replied.

"I know because many people have asked before," Mr. Bent said.

"Well, what did you tell them?" Carlos asked.

"I told them just what I shall tell you. Major City has an agreement which you must sign. This agreement says that you must divide

"If you want to begin tomorrow, you must pay $100 today."

any gold or other treasure with the city. Half to you, half to the city."

"What else?" Carlos wanted to know.

"You must pay $100 before you can begin digging or drilling," Mr. Bent said.

He handed each of them a copy of the agreement. "Pay the money and sign this. Then I'll give you the key to the gate."

"We better go outside and talk about this," P.J. said.

Once outside, he asked, "Do you have an extra hundred dollars, Carlos?"

Carlos shook his head. "No way. Do you ever remember when I had any extra money?"

P.J. put his hand in his pocket. "I'm broke, too. Let's tell Mr. Bent we'll come back later."

CHAPTER 4

More Trouble

On the Monday after the trip to the park Carlos and P.J. talked about their next move on their way home from work.

"Why don't we go there next Saturday and walk around again? Maybe we can look over the back section of the park," Carlos said.

"Carlos, hundreds of people have looked for the treasure in the park. They've never found it. What do we know that would help us find it? We don't know anything they didn't know," P.J. said.

Carlos said quickly, "You and me, we're lucky. We'll find it."

"O.K. If you want to, we'll go look again on Saturday," P.J. said.

Saturday was a nice day. Carlos and P.J. went to the park very early. The bus that carried visitors a part of the way through the park did not start until later. So they began walking slowly along the roads the bus used.

After a while they turned off the road onto trails that went into the woods.

P.J. said, "We must get off this trail. We need to look in places not many people have looked before."

"You're right. Let's head into those big trees over there," Carlos said.

"Let's get moving," P.J. said and began to jog. Carlos jogged beside him.

They soon turned off the trail and walked among large oak and elm trees. They saw more than one group of red oak trees and big rocks nearby. Any of these could be the place where the treasure had been buried.

"Hey! It was a place just like this where the book said the treasure was buried," Carlos said.

"You're right, Carlos, but there are many places in the park like this. We have to decide which one is the right place to dig," P.J. said.

"How will we do that?" Carlos wanted to know.

"I don't know yet," P.J. said. "We're just going to have to make some good plans."

Carlos nodded his head. "Yeah, and we've also got to decide if we want to pay $100 to the city."

P.J. sighed. He turned to walk back toward the bus stop. "Let's go home, Carlos. I'm tired."

"Me, too. And I'm hungry. It's long past lunch time," Carlos said.

"Next time we'll bring lunch," P.J. said.

They found a bus stop and sat down on a bench. As they sat there, they heard some noise behind them. They turned to see Bruno and Mac moving toward them.

"I don't feel like running, Carlos. Let's find out what they want," P.J. said.

Bruno and Mac walked up and stood beside the bench.

"What are you two doin'?" Bruno's voice was rough and mean.

Carlos said, "We're just visiting the park. What are you doing?"

Mac said in an angry voice. "Don't try to kid us. You're looking for the treasure. So are we."

Bruno poked Mac with his elbow. Then he said in a much nicer voice. "We think that the four of us could join and look together. That way we can find the treasure quicker. You know some things, and we know some things about the treasure. We can join and each of us will know more."

"What treasure are you talking about, Bruno?" P.J. asked.

Now Bruno spoke loudly. "Don't play games with us! We know what's going on. We know you talked with Mr. Bent about coming in the back way. It won't be safe to try to do that alone."

Mac chimed in, "Yeah. Stay healthy. Work with us."

"We'll give you a couple of days to make

Mac said in an angry voice, "You're looking for the treasure. So are we."

up your mind," Bruno said.

The park bus drove up, and P.J. and Carlos quickly got on it. Bruno and Mac stayed behind.

"Wow! I was glad to see the bus," Carlos said.

"Next time we meet those two there may not be a bus nearby," P.J. said.

"I don't want to think about that," Carlos said with a sigh.

CHAPTER 5

A New Partner

P.J. and Carlos did not know where to get $100. They talked about it the day after their park visit.

"We could ask my Uncle Munn. Sometimes he has some extra cash," Carlos said.

P.J. replied, "That's a good idea. Will we have to tell him why we want the money?"

"Oh, yes. He is curious about everything. He won't lend us two cents unless we tell him why we want the money," Carlos said.

"Is he a gambler? Does he like to bet on things?" P.J. asked.

"I don't know," Carlos said.

"Does he talk to other people a lot?" P.J. wanted to know.

"Yes. He jokes a lot with everybody," Carlos said.

"That doesn't sound good. I was thinking that we might tell him the whole story about the treasure. Maybe ask him to be a partner. If we find the treasure, he gets part of it," P.J. said.

Carlos smiled and said, "Hey! That might work. If we asked him to keep a secret, I think he would."

"Let's pay your Uncle Munn a visit," P.J. said.

Carlos called to find out if Uncle Munn was home. Aunt Val answered the phone. "Yes, he's home now. He will be glad to see you."

"We'll see you soon. We're on our way," Carlos said.

It took Carlos and P.J. about 15 minutes to reach the building where Uncle Munn and Aunt Val lived. They went up the steps, and Carlos knocked on the door.

Aunt Val opened the door. "We are very

glad to see you, Carlos, and you, too, P.J. You don't visit us very often."

"You're right. I should come by to visit more than I do. I promise to do better," Carlos said.

Uncle Munn came into the room and greeted them. He pointed to a couch and some chairs and said, "Let's sit down."

They talked for a few minutes about other members of the family.

Then Carlos took a deep breath and said, "Well, Uncle Munn, we're here to ask a favor."

"What is it, young fellow?" Uncle Munn asked.

"P.J. and I have something special we want to do. It may bring us a lot of money. Or it may bring us nothing at all. It is a chance we have to take," Carlos said.

Uncle Munn leaned back in his chair. "I have a feeling you want some money."

"Yes, sir," Carlos said.

"How much do you want?" Uncle Munn asked.

Carlos said, "We need to borrow $100."

"One hundred dollars! What do you need it for?" Uncle Munn asked.

Uncle Munn came into the room and greeted them.

"To pay fees," P.J. said.

Aunt Val smiled and looked pleased. "I think I know why you want the money. You need it to pay fees to start college."

Carlos and P.J. said nothing.

After a few moments Carlos said, "No, Aunt Val. It would take a lot more than $100 for me to start college. That's one reason I never did go."

Aunt Val replied, "I wish you would go to college, Carlos. You would learn how to do something important."

Then Carlos said, "Well, it is something important that we want to borrow the money for."

Uncle Munn repeated his question. "Why do you need the money?"

"We want to take a chance on making a lot of money," Carlos said.

"Maybe more money than we've ever seen before," P.J. said.

"You still haven't answered my question. Why do you need the money?" Uncle Munn asked.

Carlos said, "We didn't want to tell you what the money is for. We don't want other people to know what we are doing."

Uncle Munn seemed to think about the matter for a short time before he said, "You know, I agree with you. Often it is best if no one else knows what we are doing."

Carlos smiled and asked, "Then you are willing to lend us the $100?"

"Would you take me on as a partner in this mysterious job?" Uncle Munn wanted to know.

"Wow! That would be great," Carlos said.

"Sounds great to me, too. Really great," P.J. said.

"Let's shake hands on it. We will work together and share any profit we make. Now tell me all about it," Uncle Munn said.

They all stood up and shook hands. Later

they talked for a long time as they told Uncle Munn all about the treasure. Carlos and P.J. told Uncle Munn many times that there might not be any treasure at all. They felt that it was only fair that he know that.

CHAPTER 6

Gold Fever

One late afternoon Carlos and P.J. drove with Uncle Munn to the city park. They had already told him about their problems with Bruno and Mac.

They all went to Mr. Bent's office and signed the contract with Major City. Uncle Munn paid $100. The agreement said that half of any treasure found would belong to Major City and half to the treasure hunters.

Mr. Bent was helpful. He gave them a map of the woodlands and open spaces on the back side of the park where they would be allowed to search. They were not allowed to use blasting powder or similar ways to tear up the ground. Most of the work would have to be done with picks and shovels.

Mr. Bent said, "Most people who have hunted for the treasure in recent years have not been willing to work hard at it. I don't know why they wasted their money."

Uncle Munn said quickly, "I'm not paying this money just to quit when I begin to get tired. We will do a lot of hard work with shovels and picks. Then maybe we'll rent a drill and bring it in. But if treasure is buried back there, we will find it."

"Right!" Carlos and P.J. said.

The next Saturday the three treasure hunters used a key to open the back gate. After they drove through it, Carlos and P.J. closed it again.

Uncle Munn said, "I don't think we'll need the picks and shovels today. We may have to spend a lot of time looking for a spot where we want to dig. But first let's check some of the places you thought looked good."

P.J. said, "We saw five or six places that looked like the spot the book described. We also saw some other places we thought might be good for hiding treasure. But those spots didn't look anything like the one the book told about."

Uncle Munn said, "O.K. Let's get moving."

He began driving the car along the narrow gravel road through the woods. After a short drive P.J. told Uncle Munn, "Stop just ahead. We are near one of the spots where the treasure could be."

Uncle Munn stopped the car. They walked into the woods for a short distance. They stopped at the edge of a clearing in the woods. A large rock rose out of the ground at the edge of the clearing. On one side were a number of red oak trees. The rock and the red oaks had been talked about in the book.

They all got out of the car and walked around the clearing. They tried to mark with small stakes the places that might be spots for treasure to be buried.

"Now what do we do? Do we dig or do we wait?" asked Carlos.

P.J. said, "If we dig, others will know where we haven't found the treasure. They will know where NOT to dig."

Uncle Munn said softly, "That doesn't matter. We must dig any place we think the treasure might be. We don't care what others do. We will dig and then fill up the holes as the city says we must."

Carlos said, "Great! Let's not look any more. Let's just get busy."

He picked up one of the picks they had brought and began to swing it sharply against the ground. On every swing the soil was torn apart. After a few swings he moved back, and P.J. used a shovel to make a wide open hole. Uncle Munn was using another pick a few yards away.

Within an hour the three of them had dug a

trench in the soil. The trench was ten feet long and three feet deep. From time to time they stopped to rest for a few minutes. Uncle Munn had brought a large canvas sheet. They shoveled the soil they took out of the hole onto the canvas sheet. This should make it easy to fill in the hole without leaving messy mounds of dirt.

After they had dug into the ground for two or three feet, they often found solid rock.

All that morning they stayed at the same clearing in the woods. They worked very hard. They dug three trenches and filled them in again.

They were very tired by lunch time. They walked back to the car and ate there.

Carlos said in a tired voice, "I didn't know looking for treasure would be such hard work."

"Our muscles will be sore tomorrow." P.J. said with a grin.

Uncle Munn took a bite of sandwich. "I think we are doing this the hard way. Next time we'll bring along a power drill. A drill we can power with a battery. Then we can drill down into the dirt for a few feet. If we strike solid rock, we won't bother to dig with shovels. We'll move onto another spot. That way we won't waste so much time digging in the wrong places."

Carlos said, "That's a great idea. Why don't we call it a day and go home?"

P.J. replied, "First, let's drive around to some other spots where the treasure could be. Uncle Munn could get a look at some of these. He might be able to decide which of the places we should drill next time."

"Sounds good to me," said Uncle Munn.

They looked carefully at three other spots that day. They chose a spot where they would drill and dig next time they came.

It was Saturday before they could go to the park again. That morning Uncle Munn got a drill from a friend.

They went into the park through the back gate and drove along the narrow road. They parked near a level spot between rock and some trees. Here they used the drill for much of the morning. It made a very loud noise.

They were not so tired at lunch that day. While sitting in the car and eating their lunches, they saw Bruno and Mac coming toward them.

P.J. said to Uncle Munn, "Here come the two fellows who caused us some trouble. Remember? We told you about them the other day."

"I remember. Let's get out of the car and be polite," Uncle Munn said.

The three of them got out of the car and watched Bruno and Mac walk toward them.

"Hello. Are you having a nice walk?" Uncle Munn asked as Bruno and Mac walked up to them.

"Hello. Yes, we are having a very nice walk. We found you three," Bruno said.

"Why did you want to find us, Bruno?" P.J. asked.

"You know why. We've told you before," Mac said.

Uncle Munn said softly to them, "Well, you haven't told ME. I'm new in this work with P.J. and Carlos. Tell me why you needed to find us."

"We're gonna help these two look for treasure. We think they need help," Mac said in an angry voice.

Uncle Munn turned to P.J. and Carlos. "Did you invite these nice fellows to help you look for anything you might be looking for?"

"No, we did not," Carlos said.

Uncle Munn took off the jacket he was wearing. He laid it across the hood of his car. Then he removed his cap and laid it on top of the jacket.

Uncle Munn's arms were large with big muscles. It was easy to see that he was a very strong man.

Uncle Munn took a few practice swings in the air in front of him. Then he turned to Bruno and Mac.

"Why don't you continue your nice walk through the park? We don't need help," he said.

Mac said, "You think you can bully us with your big, fat muscles. We're not afraid. You aren't gonna chase us away."

Uncle Munn walked over to Bruno and Mac. He asked Bruno, "Do you agree with your friend?"

Bruno was slow to answer. Then he said. "I don't think we need to fight about it. We just wanted to help."

Mac turned to Bruno and said loudly, "Are you afraid of that old man? Maybe he is big but he's old. I can tear him apart in two minutes!"

Bruno thought for a few seconds. Then he said, "I don't think you want to fight that man, Mac. Let's go on with our walk."

Mac said loudly, "Go on with your walk,

you coward. I'm going to show this old guy how to fight."

"I think you're gonna be sorry," Bruno said as he walked away.

Uncle Munn said softly, "Young man, I don't want to fight. Walk along with your friend."

Mac made a sudden rush toward Uncle Munn. When he got close, he swung his fist toward Uncle Munn's face.

Uncle Munn moved his right hand in front of his face. He grabbed Mac's fist and made a fast twist with it. The movement of his hand was so quick and so strong that Mac was turned completely around. Uncle Munn was holding Mac's arm behind his back in a painful way. Mac tried to pull himself free but he could not.

"Turn me loose, you big bully!" Mac yelled.

"Is the fight over?" Uncle Munn wanted to know.

Mac did not answer. He just kept breathing hard and struggling.

Uncle Munn waited a few seconds. Then he gave Mac a slight push forward.

"Go with your friend," he said sharply to

The movement of his hand was so quick and strong that Mac turned completely around.

Mac. Mac stumbled down the path.

Uncle Munn turned back to the car. "Shall we go home?" he asked P.J. and Carlos.

"You bet!" they said.

CHAPTER 7

The Treasure!

P.J., Carlos, and Uncle Munn went back to the park every Saturday and sometimes on days in between. They drilled and dug.

Uncle Munn took time off from his job whenever he could. Then they all drilled and dug, dug and drilled.

One summer day in the park P.J. said, "Carlos, I don't think there's any gold here. We're wasting our time."

Carlos said, "You may be right, P.J., but I've found one good thing."

"What's that?" P.J. asked.

Carlos held out his arms and moved them up and down. I've found big muscles," he said.

They both laughed.

"Let's drill here," Carlos said. He pointed to a level spot between two small groups of trees.

"O.K. But let's make this our last drill for today. I want to go somewhere for a nice cold drink," P.J. said.

"Me, too," said Carlos as he moved the drill to a level place and turned on the power. He pushed harder, and the bit went deeper into the ground.

After a few minutes Carlos stopped the drill and said to P.J., "This is a good spot to dig. The drill didn't hit any rocks."

"O.K. Then I'll start digging," P.J. said. He took the pick to loosen the ground. Carlos spread the big canvas sheet on the ground. He grabbed a shovel and lifted loose dirt onto the sheet.

Next, P.J. and Carlos dug a narrow ditch a few feet into the ground. P.J. began to strike small stones.

"This looks like another wrong place, Carlos," he said.

"Keep digging. We haven't hit solid rock yet," Carlos said.

P.J. swung the pick again and again. Carlos moved the shovel deeper and deeper. Suddenly P.J. stopped. "Carlos, my last swing hit something solid," he said.

Carlos was hot and tired. "If it's more rock, we'll go get that cold drink."

P.J. replied, "I don't think it was rock my pick hit. Maybe it was just a piece of wood in the dirt."

P.J. swung the pick up and down to make the dirt loose. Carlos quickly jumped into the hole. He pushed his shovel into the dirt. He reached up and emptied his shovel onto the canvas. After he did this a few times, he dropped the shovel and fell onto one knee. He used his hands to push the dirt away.

"Wow! There's something here. I don't

know what it is yet," he said.

He began moving the shovel very fast. In a short time he stopped and stared at the top of a broad metal box. He looked as if he couldn't believe his eyes. "What have we found? What have we found?" he asked

P.J. jumped into the hole. He swung the pick into the firm dirt around the box. Carlos moved the loose dirt out with his shovel. Then they each grabbed an end of the box and lifted it out of the hole.

Carlos was yelling, "Wow! Wow!" over and over again.

At first P.J. made no sound. He just stood there staring at the box. Then he tried to open it. It would not open. He grabbed a rock and beat it against the metal hinges until they broke. He and Carlos pulled open the top of the box. There was something inside. They did not know what.

Carlos reached into the box. He grabbed onto some dark pieces of metal. He held them up for P.J. to see.

P.J. sat down on the ground. "I can't believe it! We found it, Carlos! We found it!" He dug one hand into the box and pulled out a few gold coins.

"What are those?" Carlos asked in wonder.

P.J. said slowly, "Spanish doubloons, I think. I've seen pictures of them."

"Are they really gold?" Carlos asked.

"I think so," P.J. said. "And that means they are very valuable."

"Yippee!" Carlos yelled.

A loud voice came from behind them. "Raise your hands! I have a gun."

They froze, then turned and saw Uncle Munn with his finger pointed toward them.

They all laughed together. They looked dazed as they touched and lifted the gold coins.

P.J. had a sudden thought. "Let's count the coins. We need to know how many we found. Then we must take them somewhere for safekeeping."

"You're right. We must do that quickly. Put all the coins back into the box," Uncle Munn said.

They turned and saw Uncle Munn with his finger pointed toward them.

Carlos laughed. "Can't I hold onto just a few of them and dream?"

P.J. said, "No, Carlos. We must count them. Let's do it together."

They sat down and counted.

The next few days were full of excitement. They hired Dr. Wills, a coin expert. He told them how much the coins were worth. He also told them where to sell them.

The mayor asked Dr. Wills to sell the city's share of the coins. After talking about it, Uncle Munn, Carlos, and P.J. decided to sell theirs, too. They would each get about $3,000.

"Well, rich man Carlos, what will you do with your money?" P.J. asked.

Carlos said, "I've been thinking about that. I may make Aunt Val happy and look into college. What about you, P.J.?"

P.J. smiled. "Who knows? I may do the college thing with you. But I also want to donate some books about treasure hunting to the library. After all, it was a library book that started us out on a treasure hunt!"

Carlos laughed. "That's a great idea, P.J., but I don't know who will read them. The Major City treasure has already been found. Hey, maybe we ought to check out some more books and learn about other treasures that haven't been found yet."

P.J. just looked at him. "Oh, no," he said.